The Cat with the Crooked Tail

Dedicated to the original, beloved

ONCE UPON A

The Cat with the Crooked Tail

A Dance-It-Out Creative Movement Story for Young Movers

Illustrated by Olha Tkachenko, www.littlebig.me
Book sales from *The Cat with the Crooked Tail* donated to animal welfare organizations.
(And all 2021 book sales double donated to ballet companies struggling under COVID-19.)

Each Dance-It-Out! story is an independent kids' dance performance for the imagination stage. This volume highlights the value of practice, friendship, and a good attitude. Merida Brown thinks her tail hinders her abilities; with help from a friend, she proves herself wrong. Ballerina Konora helps readers connect with storytelling, body coordination, and dance fundamentals.

LCCN: 2021915192 ISBN 978-1-9555-5504-3 (paperback); 978-1-9555-5505-0 (ebook); 978-1-955555-06-7 (hardcover)

Juvenile Fiction: Animals: Cats
(Juvenile Fiction: Imagination & Play; Juvenile Fiction: Social Themes: New Experience; Juvenile Fiction: Performing Arts: Dance)

First Edition

Dance-It-Out! Series, Dancing Shapes Series, and Other *Once Upon a Dance* Titles:
Joey Finds His Jump!: A Dance-It-Out Creative Movement Story for Young Movers
Petunia Perks Up: A Dance-It-Out Movement and Meditation Story
Danny, Denny, and the Dancing Dragon: A Dance-It-Out Creative Movement Story for Young Movers
Princess Naomi Helps a Unicorn: A Dance-It-Out Creative Movement Story for Young Movers
Brielle's Birthday Ball: A Dance-It-Out Creative Movement Story for Young Movers
Mira Monkey's Magic Mirror Adventure: A Dance-It-Out Creative Movement Story for Young Movers
Belluna's Big Adventure in the Sky: A Dance-It-Out Creative Movement Story for Young Movers
Freya, Fynn, and the Fantastic Flute A Dance-It-Out Creative Movement Story for Young Movers
Danika's Dancing Day: A Dance-It-Out Creative Movement Story for Young Movers
Sadoni Squirrel: Superhero: A Dance-It-Out Creative Movement Story for Young Movers
Dancing Shapes: Ballet and Body Awareness for Young Dancers
More Dancing Shapes: Ballet and Body Awareness for Young Dancers
Nutcracker Dancing Shapes: Shapes and Stories from Konora's Twenty-Five Nutcracker Roles
Dancing Shapes with Attitude: Ballet and Body Awareness for Young Dancers
Konora's Shapes: Poses from Dancing Shapes for Creative Movement & Ballet Teachers
More Konora's Shapes: Poses from More Dancing Shapes for Creative Movement & Ballet Teachers
Ballerina Dreams Ballet Inspiration Journal/Notebook
Dancing Shapes Ballet Inspiration Journal/Notebook

Hello Fellow Dancer,

My name is Ballerina Konora.

I love stories, adventures, and ballet.

I'm glad you're here with me!

Will you be my dance partner and act out this story with me and Merida? I've included descriptions of movements that express the story. You can decide whether to use these ideas or create your own moves.

Be safe, of course, and do what works for you in your space. And if you'd rather settle in and enjoy the pictures the first time through, that's fine, too.

Konora

P.S. Boy or girl, you can move like all the kitty characters in this story, and of course, feel free to create the shapes and story that work for your body. Dance is for everybody!

Once upon a dance, there was a little farm cat named Miss Merida Brown. Her family gave her a brave name because she was so tiny and timid. Not only was she small, she was also partially bald. Her tabby-brown fur showed only in patches. Her tail was a little shorter than most of the other cats', and it was crooked.

Let's pretend to be a little kitty on hands and knees. We can make Merida Brown's crooked tail by putting one bent leg in the air behind us. It doesn't look exactly like Merida's, but it's close enough.

As she grew, Merida got stronger and her fur grew in, but her tail stayed crooked. Sometimes if she focused all her power into her tail, she could make it straight, but the new shape only lasted for a second or two.

Her tail didn't stop her from being a kind kitty and a good friend. Merida loved rubbing noses with all the other cats, and she always wanted to be where they were.

We'll extend that bent kitty tail into a straight leg. One leg to the back is seen so often in ballet, it has its own ballet name: *arabesque.*

Next, imagine rubbing noses with the other cats. Maybe find a stuffed animal or willing person to share your kitty greeting.

There were many cats on the farm. Most of them spent sunny days perched on a ladder or resting in another high-up spot of sunshine. Merida wasn't sure she could keep her balance, so she often sat alone below.

Even though she said nothing, she secretly blamed her crooked tail.

First, let's act out a slightly sad Merida on the ground looking up at her friends. If you want, you could be like the other cats by using a rolled-up towel or blanket, or a chain of building blocks (maybe get a grown-up's help), and practice walking and sitting on your *balance beam.*

On rainy days, the cats used the barn as one giant obstacle course. They would spend hours climbing, jumping, crawling, balancing, and squeezing through tight spaces.

Merida lay curled up in the corner, hoping no one would notice her.

For our obstacle course (if it's okay with your grown-up), you could get a box to crawl through or a chair to crawl under. Use some post-it notes or tape to jump from spot to spot. You could stack some books or other small objects to step over. For hammock practice, you could put ribbons or yarn on the floor like a tic-tac-toe board and try to step in the holes. You can add your own ideas, too.

One day, Merida's best friend Ziggy asked her why she never played on the obstacle course.

"I always fall because of my tail," said Merida.

"Oh, I didn't realize you'd tried it," said Ziggy.

"I haven't," said Merida, "but my tail makes me not good at things like that. Look, I can't even balance on two legs." She attempted to reach out one arm and one leg. Then she went splat on her belly.

"I think you just need some training," said Ziggy.

Merida's balance move seems pretty tricky, but we can give it a try. Get on your hands and knees and reach one arm forward. Come back to hands and knees, and reach one leg out behind you, just a little off the ground. If those worked out all right, try one arm and the leg on the opposite side at the same time. It's okay if you fall like Merida. Keep practicing!

Ziggy took Merida outside. He found places for her to practice similar obstacles with no one watching. They walked across sticks on the ground, squeezed through a hole in the fence, jumped from stump to stump, and climbed up the clothes on the clothesline. They didn't have a hammock, but Merida practiced walking on a table with lots of holes.

"Do you think I'm ready?" Merida asked.

"Yes, but either way, it doesn't matter," said Ziggy. "We're your friends. Besides, most of us fell the first time."

Merida seemed surprised by this. But once she thought about it, she realized it was true. Cats often fell, and Merida never thought badly about them. Why should they think less of her? She gave Ziggy a kitty high-five and a huge grin.

So, it's not a kitty gesture, but we could keep our elbows next to our bodies as we reach out our arms palms up and lift our shoulders like we're asking a question. And we can show we are thinking by tilting our heads and tapping a finger to our forehead. Then high-five your stuffed animal, imaginary friend, or someone nearby, and give them a happy smile.

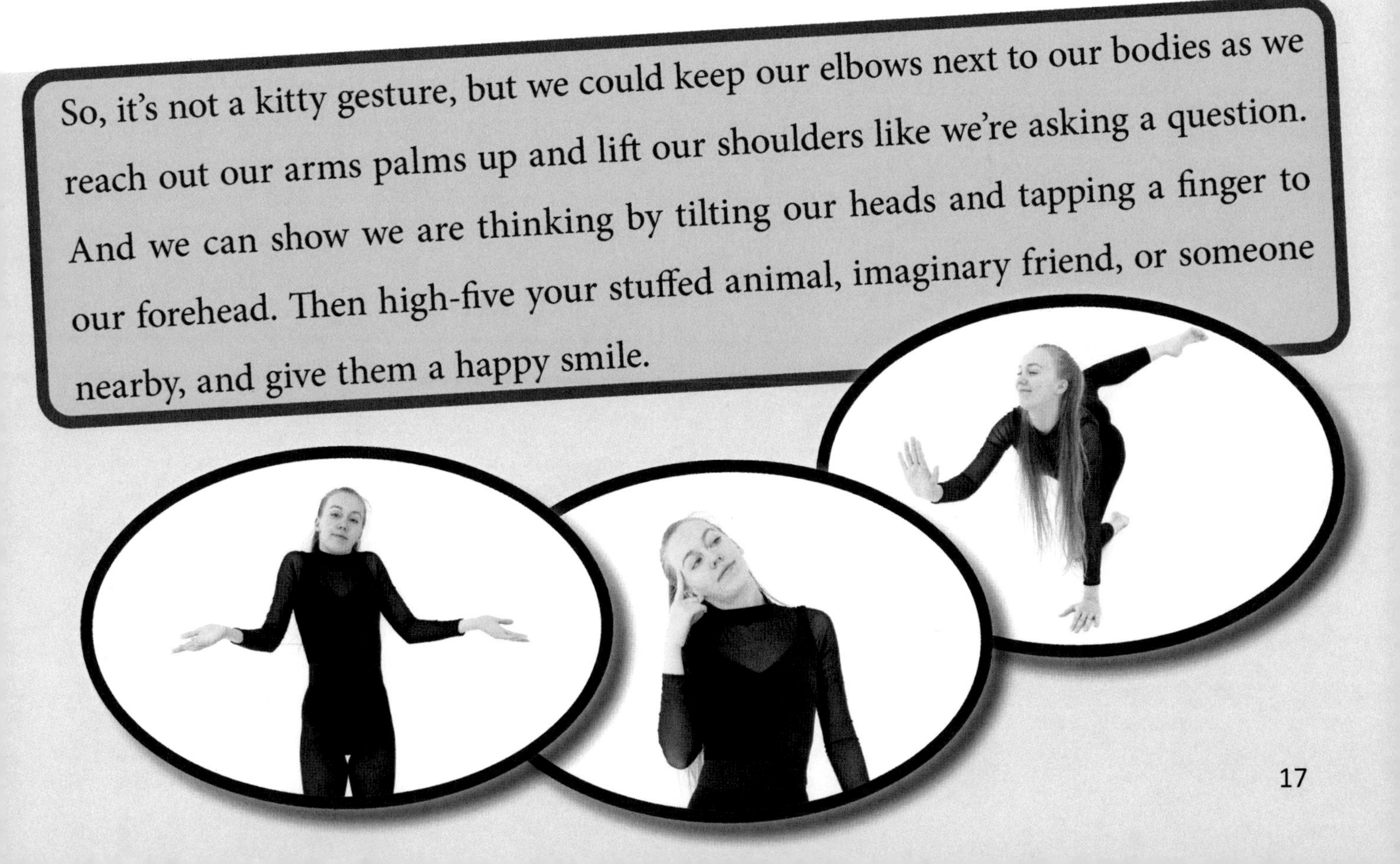

The very next rainy day, Merida tried the obstacle course. She felt confident she could handle the first parts. The only obstacle that worried her was the hammock.

When it was her turn, Merida took a deep breath and took off. She made it up the flag, through the holes, across the beam, and through the jumps. Only the hammock was left. Would she make it?

Maybe add one thing that feels tricky to our obstacle course for our third time around. You could make a taller stack of books to leap over, or put the stepping-stone post-it notes farther apart. Take a nice, deep breath before you begin.

Whoooaa! She tried to keep her balance, but nope. Ker-splat! She made a gloriously awkward fall right onto her backside!

She looked around. No one laughed. A couple of cats, including Ziggy, came over to make sure she wasn't hurt. They told her she'd done a great job with the other obstacles.

Feeling more confident than ever, Merida got back up, dusted herself off, and got in line to try the entire course again.

Let's re-create the moment before the fall. Try to keep your balance with arms extended and moving all around, and shifting the top half of your body in every direction. Bend your knees, get lower to the ground and fall sideways, trying to roll a little as you hit the ground.

Let's turn our heads side to side to see if anyone's laughing. Then, like Merida, we'll stand up, brush away the pretend dust from our bellies, hips, thighs, knees, and feet and triumphantly decide to try again.

The second try, Merida made it! She and Ziggy rubbed noses, and her friends clapped and cheered. And just like that, she wasn't afraid of trying new things. She still figured her tail made her not as good at balancing and leaping as the other cats, but she felt a lot better. From that moment on, her crooked tail was always just a bit higher in the air.

Merida spent the whole day hanging out in line and taking turns on the obstacle course. Even though she felt more confident, she fell off again her fourth time around. As she hit the ground, she realized how happy she was just being part of the group and having fun. She laughed at how silly she'd been to miss out because she was afraid of embarrassing herself.

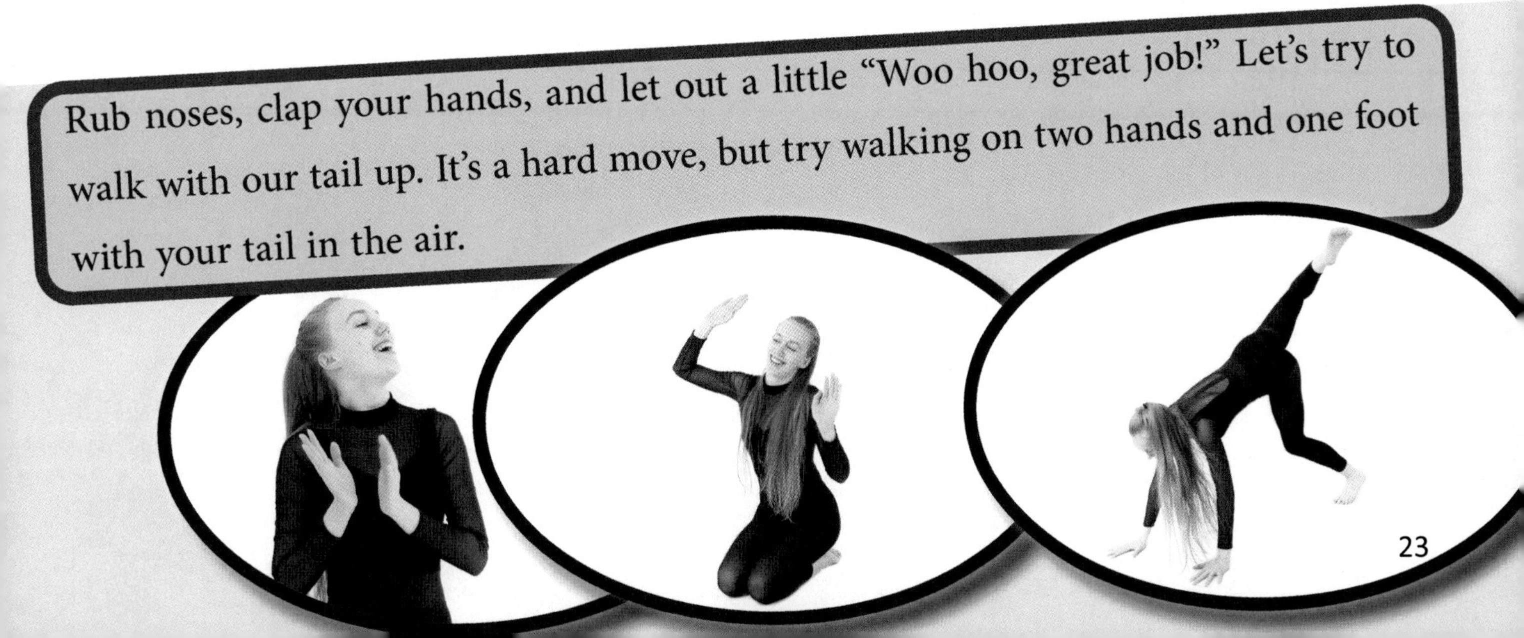

The very next day, a new family of cats came to visit. They were welcomed with a day of obstacle-course celebrations.

The first cat tried climbing up the flag. Splat! The next one got up the flag but fell off the boards. And the one after that spun around in the hammock and fell out in a dizzy stumble. None of the cats seemed to mind falling off. Some even laughed as they picked themselves up and brushed the dust away.

Let's imagine we're that orange kitty. We try to pull ourselves up with our arms, then do a slow-motion fall by bending our knees and squatting down low so we can gently sit down and roll onto our backs. For the cat-on-the-hammock spin, let's start with one arm above the other in front of us and circle our hands round and round each other. How fast can you circle your arms without them touching?

The new cats took turns. It seemed like every other time Merida looked, a cat was landing on its bottom or all fours.

Merida did a double take when she noticed a cat without a tail. He made it across the hammock and started doing the coolest tricks! While still holding on, he flipped the hammock upside down, hung by his front legs, and lifted his hind legs in opposite directions. Then he let go with one paw and was barely holding on. Merida turned her head and looked away in fear.

Let's combine a fall with a half spin. Start standing, then bend your knees to squat, and twist and reach behind you as you spin halfway around, belly facing down. Reach for the ground to land on your hands and feet. Fancy!

We'll take a giant step and imagine we're hanging with our legs stretched out. We'll put one arm down to match the cat-with-no-tail's pose (let's call him Stubby).

Finally, we can pretend to be Merida hiding her eyes and twisting away.

Her friends all started cheering. The cat with no tail was spinning under the hammock while holding on with only one paw at a time. He spun himself all the way to one end, and then started spinning the other direction to come back.

To do Stubby's spinning trick, reach your arms up in the air. If you've seen monkey bars at the park, imagine you're crossing those. It's like climbing a sideways ladder. See if you can keep reaching forward, one hand at a time, and add in a spin as you hold on.

As if performing a finale, the cat with no tail flipped his legs up and over the hammock and the entire hammock started spinning around. Then he let go, sailed up into the air, did a little kick, and landed gracefully a few feet from Merida.

We can lie down and lift our legs up in the air the way Stubby gets started. Then circle your arms around each other again for the hammock spin. For the kick, I'm going to send one leg behind me as I reach for the ground. Can you think of another idea?

We humans should use our legs to land. Try a frog-style or regular jump.

Merida's mouth hung open. "How did you learn to do that?" she asked.

"Practice. One of my friends has a family with a hammock and a swing-set." Then he whispered, "Want to visit sometime?"

Merida smiled wide, nodded, and told him she'd love to. She expected hammock training might involve more falling, but she still couldn't wait to try.

Let's stretch our mouths open. (I find I immediately yawn when I do.) Give a nice, silly smile and nod your head by reaching your forehead up to the ceiling and then lower your chin down to your chest.

Thee end!
The end.

(My grandpa always ended stories this way, and I like to share the fun.)

Thank you for being my dance partner!

Until our next adventure,

Love, *Konora*

Konora's Kitties

Miss Merida Brown (her actual name) was our dearest kitty of many beloved cats (we currently have five). Merida was tiny and timid, and she only had three legs. She was sick when we adopted her, and we knew she wouldn't be with us very long. The owner who had Merida before had too many cats and didn't take good care of them so people took the cats away so they could get better homes. Merida was scared at first, but with patience and love, she grew braver and loved her new home. She adored my mother and always wanted to be in her lap.

Cosette had the bald patches. She came from another sad previous-owner situation. Cosette's eyes watered for months, and the vet said there was nothing wrong with them. It felt like she was crying. Her fur grew in and she gets braver every day. She LOVES belly rubs, but she's still getting used to us.

Lucy's the one with the crooked tail, which is better than Finney who only has a stub for a tail. Neither Lucy nor Finney ever let their tails slow them down.

Finney's now my cat and he's traveled with me as I've moved from city to city chasing my ballet dreams. He's a tough guy and seems to enjoy adventure. Even though he's old enough to be a grandpa cat, you'd never know it. I could totally see him conquering the kitty obstacle course. 😉

A few of our feline friends
Lucy
Miss Merida Brown
Finney
Cosette (Before & After)
Jez
Halo
Dudley
Pandora

GIVE US A KITTY GRIN?

We check for new reviews daily and would be grateful for a kind, honest review at Amazon or Goodreads. *The Cat with the Crooked Tail* is a mother-daughter COVID-collaboration. We were both immersed in the ballet world until the pandemic, and it took a lot of learning to publish this book. We really hope you like it, check out our other books, and tell your friends who might enjoy it.

Grown-ups can visit
www.OnceUponADance.com
for bonus content and information on upcoming books.

The Dance-it-Out! Collection

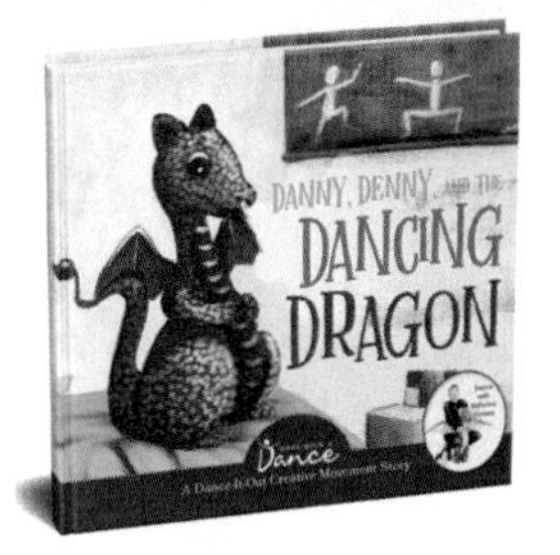

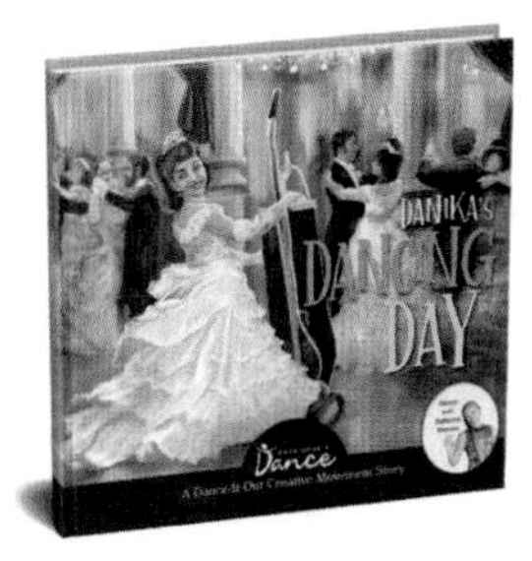

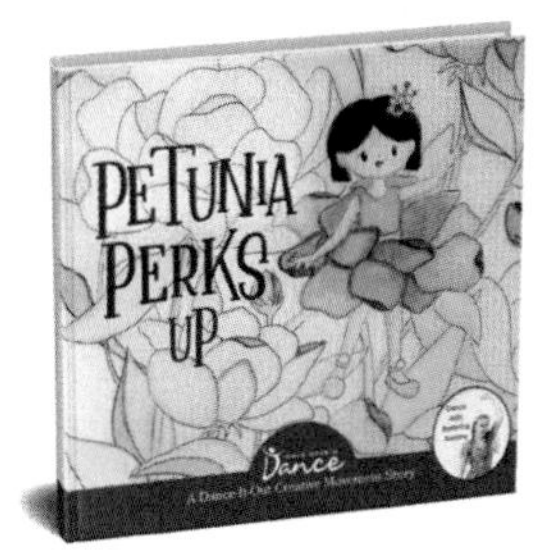

Series catalog also includes:

Dancing Shapes · Konora's Shapes · Ballet Journals

www.OnceUponADance.com

Watch for Subscriber Bonus Content

Here's a bonus challenge pose.
One photo in the book was taken on a different day. Do you want to guess which photo?

Made in the USA
Middletown, DE
19 December 2021